Halloween Mice!

Halloween Mice!

by Bethany Roberts

Illustrated by Doug Cushman

Green Light Readers
HOUGHTON MIFFLIN HARCOURT
Boston New York

The Library of Congress has cataloged the hardcover edition as follows:
Roberts, Bethany.
Halloween Mice!/by Bethany Roberts; illustrated by Doug Cushman
p. cm.
Summary: Mice whirling and skipping on Halloween night are threatened by an
approaching cat, until they come up with a scary trick to defend themselves.
[1. Mice—Fiction. 2. Cats—Fiction. 3. Halloween—Fiction.]
I Cushman, Doug, ill. II. Title
Pz7.R5396Hal 1994
[E]—dc20 93-17192

ISBN: 978-0-395-67064-4 hardcover
ISBN: 978-0-395-86619-1 paperback
ISBN: 978-0-547-57573-5 board book
ISBN: 978-0-544-23276-1 GLR paperback
ISBN: 978-0-544-23279-2 GLR paper over board

Manufactured in China
SCP 10 9 8 7 6 5 4 3

4500536950

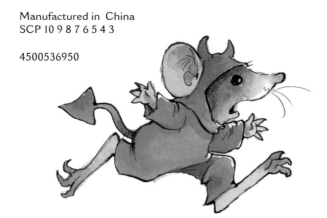

To Anne, who gave me my first Halloween mouse
—love and thanks
—B.R.

For Tony Kramer
—D.C.

Halloween mice tiptoe, tiptoe.
One little mouse is oh so slow.

Hurry! Scurry!
Frisk, frisk!

Halloween mice skitter through the cornfield.

Ghosts! Witches!
Whisk, whisk!

Halloween mice scamper in the pumpkin patch.

Having a party!
Whirl, whirl!

Halloween mice are midnight dancers,

swirling in the moonlight.
Twirl, twirl!

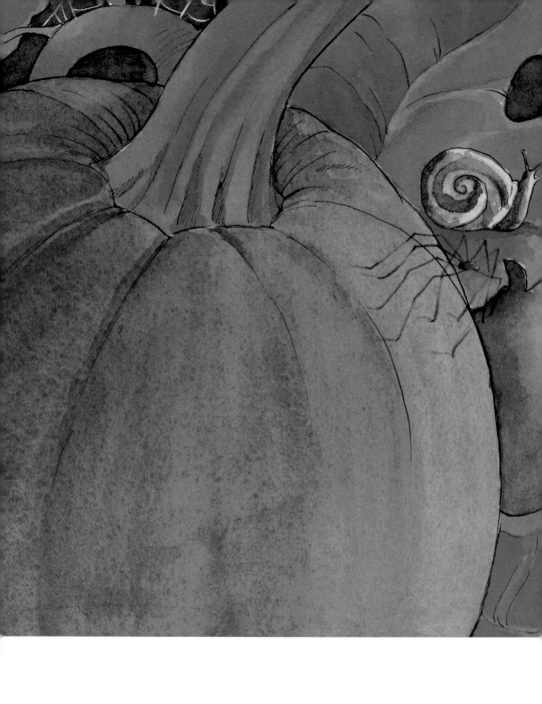

Dance, prance, round and round.

Faster! Faster!
Whish, whish!

Halloween mice stop, listen . . .

Rustle! Rustle!
Swish, swish!

Halloween cat, coming, coming . . .

Huddle, whisper!
Quick, quick!

Halloween mice make a plan.

Scramble up a pumpkin!
Click, click!

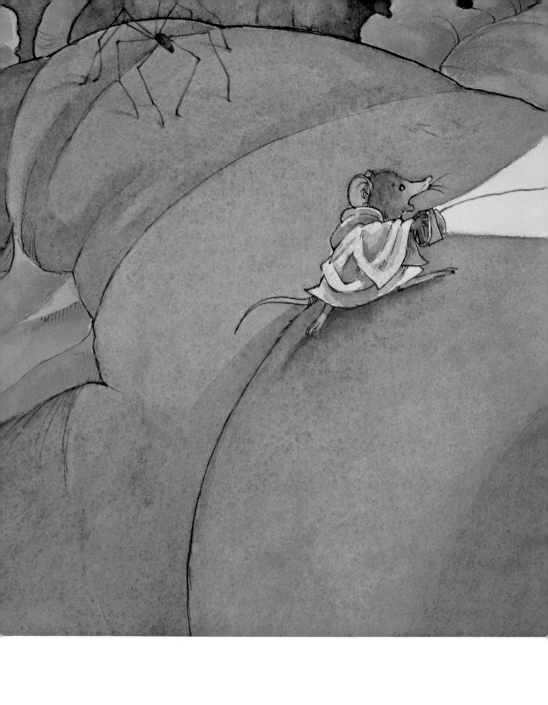

Halloween mice make a shadow.

Spooky, scary!

RUN, CAT, RUN!

Cat is gone!
Sing, swing!

Nibble on pumpkin seeds.
Yum, yum, yum!

Halloween mice tiptoe home now.

Yawning, tired.
Ho-ho-hum!

Halloween mice tumble into bed,
while Owl in the tree hoots,
Whoo! Whoo!

One little mouse still wants to party.
Waits 'til it's quiet,
then shouts . . .

"BOO!"